CARS
GALORE

Peter Stein

illustrated by Bob Staake

CANDLEWICK PRESS

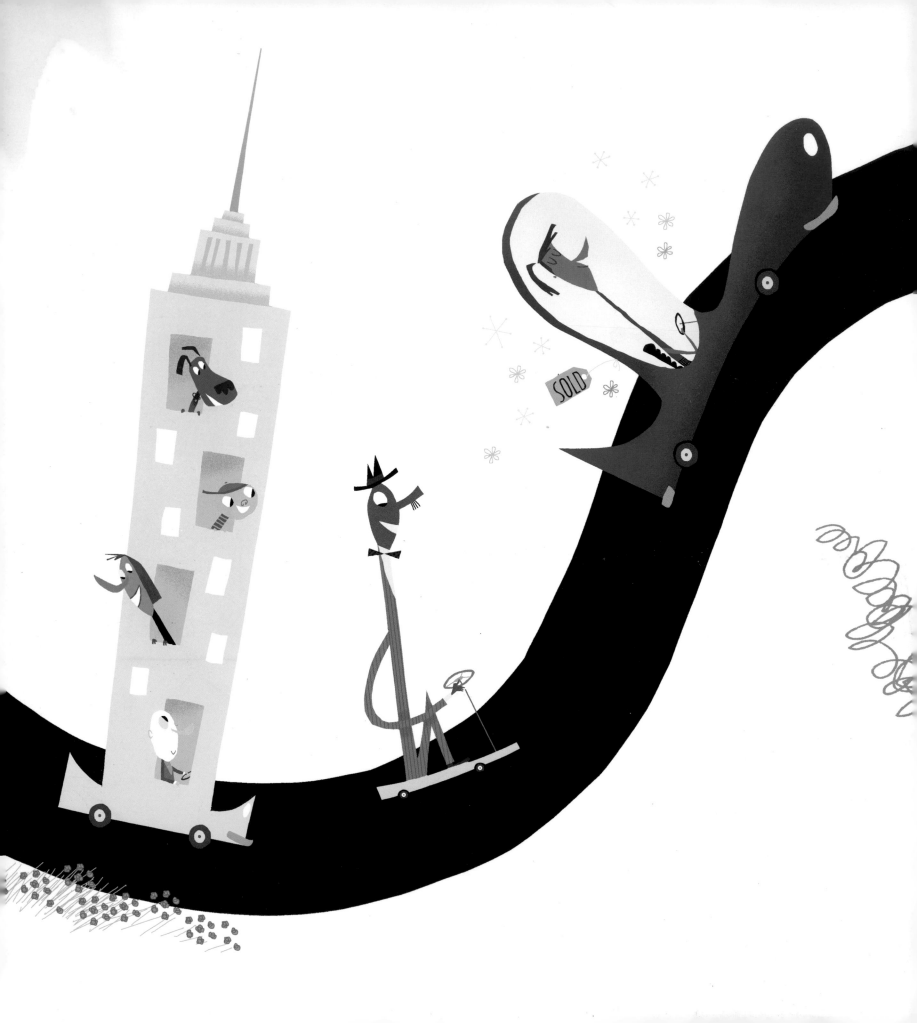

Tall car, short car,
fun-filled fort car.
New car, old car.
Has-a-cold car!

Jazz car, soul car,
rock 'n' roll car.
Blues car, song car.
Sing-along car!

Cars on highways!
Cars on cliffs!
Cars on skyways!
Cars on lifts!

Hundred-feet car.
Incomplete car.
Scary shark car.
Noah's Ark car!

Plug-in autos.
Solar autos.
Igloo ice-fueled
polar autos!

Eco-friendly,
runs-on-air car!
Zzzip-around-
without-a-care car!

Cars and cars and
yet still MORE cars!
Millions, billions,
cars-GALORE cars!

Honk cars! BEEP cars!
At-a-creep cars!
Miles of piles of
in-a-heap cars!

Cars off-roading,
jumping, thumping!
Gears all grinding!
Pistons pumping!

Cars for racing!
Cars with might!
Cars for chasing!
Hold on tight!

Rusty, dusty,
hunk-of-junk car.
Stinky, yucky,
smells-like-skunk car.

Save it! Tow it!
Big repair job!
Take-a-bath-and-
rinse-with-care job!

Quick drive, ICK drive!
Makes-you-sick drive!
Round and round drive!
Upside-down drive!

CAUTION
ICK
ROAD

But shhh . . .

This car's snoozing.
That car's snoring.
Done with cruising.
Truly boring.

Pack-it-up-and-
take-a-trip car!
Crank-it-up-and-
let-'er-rip car!

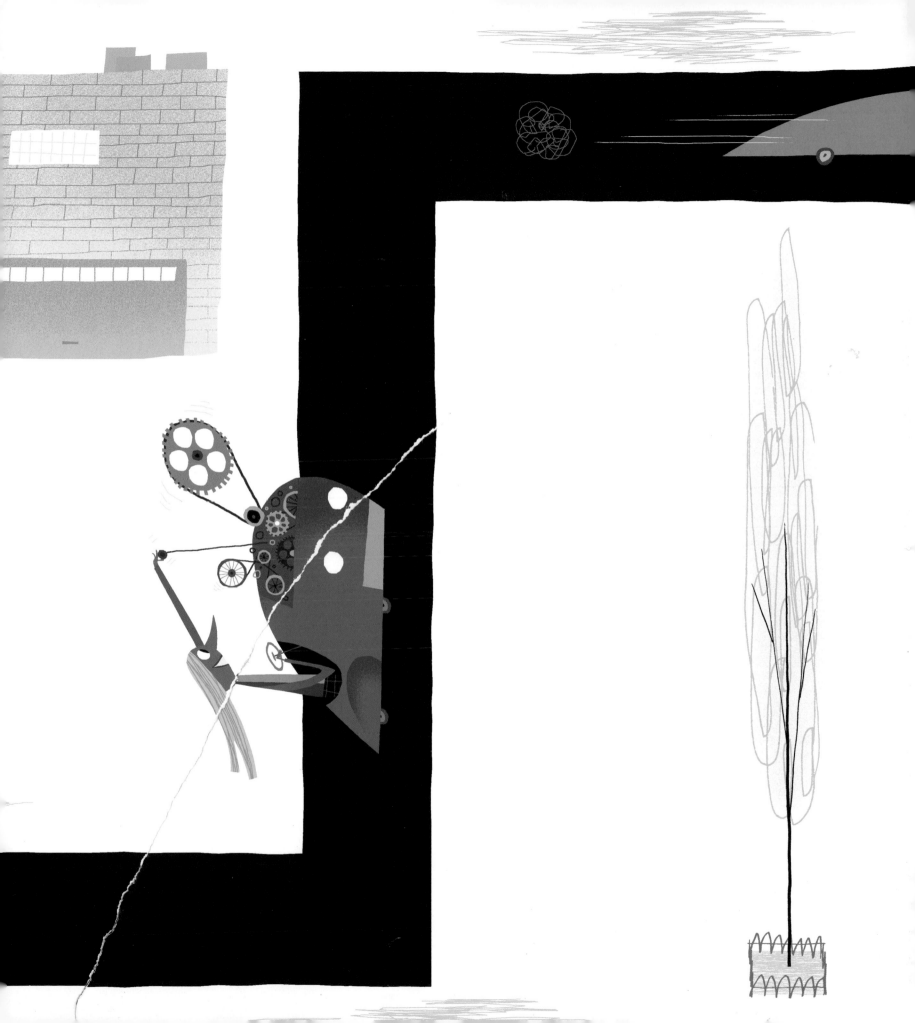

Fun drive, sun drive,
Gotta-run drive!
Dream drive, cool drive . . .

Someday
YOU'LL
drive!

For Gabriel and Elias,
my favorite backseat drivers
P. S.

For Nicole and Kelli
B. S.

Text copyright © 2011 by Peter Stein
Illustrations copyright © 2011 by Bob Staake

First edition 2011

Library of Congress Cataloging-in-Publication Data is available.

Library of Congress Catalog Card Number 2010038923

ISBN 978-0-7636-4743-8

13 14 15 16 CCP 10 9 8 7 6 5 4

Printed in Shenzhen, Guangdong, China

This book was typeset in Zalderdash.
The illustrations were done digitally.

Candlewick Press
99 Dover Street
Somerville, Massachusetts 02144

visit us at www.candlewick.com